THE SPINDLE WHORL

AN ACTIVITY BOOK

Ages 9–12

BY NAN MCNUTT

ILLUSTRATED BY ROGER FERNANDES
CENTRAL COAST SALISH ART BY SUSAN POINT AND ROGER FERNANDES

Thank you for sharing your knowledge and time that others might experience and understand. We raise our hands to you.

THANK YOU!

Vy Hilbert
Bill and Fran James
Gina Grant
Bruce Miller
Bill Holm
Michael Kew
Steve Brown
Wayne Suttles
Crisca Bierwart
Carolyn Marr
Randy Buchard
Dorothey Kennedy
Karen James
Astrida Onat
Roy Carlson

THANK YOU!

Karen Holm and the 4th and 8th graders of The Evergreen School
Steve Chavez, Faith Childs–Davis, Rick Lemberg and the 3rd, 4th, 5th and 6th graders of A.E.II Decatur Elementary School

THANK YOU!

Carvers and Spinners of the Coast! Your whorls sing strong songs.

Design by Kate Basart

SASQUATCH BOOKS
SEATTLE

Sulsuliya stops spinning. She listens to the early morning darkness of the house. "Did you hear anything, Curly Tail?" she whispers to her woolly white dog. Its tail whips against the blanket woven from dog's wool. "I've got to finish spinning this wool. It's a gift for Uncle's new wife." She listens again, but only the soft sleeping sounds of the house reach her ears.

Sulsuliya takes up her spindle and begins rolling the shaft down her leg. There is nothing more pleasurable to her than spinning fluffy wool around her little spindle, with its special whorl that spins round and round. It was the first whorl her older brother ever carved. He gave it to her after her naming ceremony. Father and Mother had hosted a large party and Grandmother had announced her adult name, Sulsuliya. It was her great aunt's name and means "spinning woman."

1

Sulsuliya **S**hears **S**sounds again. Quickly, she shakes her little sister. "Shhh," she whispers. "I think I hear Brother on the beach. Let's go see what he's up to." Quietly, the girls adjust their cedar bark skirts and capes and slip out the door.

2

Waves lap gently against the beach as gray light marks the separation between water and sky. Brother is nowhere on the beach. Then they hear the noise again, this time from the side of the house.

"I wonder if he is working on a gift, too?" whispers Little Sister. Both girls peer around the side of the house.

3

There, sitting on a log, is their older brother, carving a new spindle whorl with his beaver-tooth knife.

"What are you doing carving in the dark!" exclaims Sulsuliya, startling her brother. "You can hardly see where your knife is going!"

Brother laughs. "Look who's talking. Did I hear a mouse spinning earlier this morning? Besides, the whorl's design is already carved. I'm just hollowing out a little extra wood from the bowl of the whorl."

"Are you making a gift, too?' asks Little Sister.

Brother beams. "Well, Squirt, how do you think Uncle's wife will like it?" He holds up his newly finished whorl for their approval.

"What is that animal?" asks Little Sister.

Brother grins at her. "What do you think it might be?"

Sulsuliya smiles. She remembers the time she asked Grandmother about the images on the large old spindle whorl. Grandmother's only reply was, "What do you think it might be?"

But before Little Sister can answer Brother, the dogs begin to whine and whimper. "Oh dear, the dogs! We'd better go feed them," says Sulsuliya. "Mother wants to shear all the dogs today before Uncle comes."

Sulsuliya and Little
Sister spread
cedar bark mats
in a patch of early
sunlight. Sulsuliya
leans toward an
older dog with
a wagging
curly tail. "Are
you ready to
get rid of all
that woolly
fur, Old One?"

Others join them to help with the dogs. Mother and Auntie bring their sharp
mussel-shell knives. As they swiftly cut the wool from the dogs, it falls in soft
mounds onto the mats. Sulsuliya loves the fluffy wool. She imagines herself
spinning mountain goat wool with a large whorl. There is a special image carved
on this large whorl, but she cannot see what it is. Her mind drifts to the coming
of Uncle and his new wife.

S ulsuliya,"
her cousin nudges her,
"what are you thinking about? You look as though you're in another place."

"Oh! Oh!" stammers Sulsuliya. Embarrassed, she giggles, "I was just wondering if Uncle and his new wife might come today. I hope our gifts of yarn and blankets will please them."

Her cousin teases, "You are always thinking about wool. Why last night in your sleep you were holding the tassels of your blanket and spinning them!"

Sulsuliya blushes and laughs. They all laugh together.

Hooooo! Hoooooo!" a deep loud voice sings out across the inlet waters. Sulsuliya and her family rush out to see who calls to them. Several canoes are approaching the beach, and a man in a long white robe is standing in the lead canoe. He raises his arm in a greeting to Sulsuliya's village. "We ask permission to come to the house of my brother-in-law!" rings out the deep voice.

"Look, there's Uncle! And that must be his new wife!" Little Sister points to a woman not much older than Sulsuliya. She too is dressed in a white robe and is sitting high in the canoe. All the men and women in the other canoes, some paddlers and some drummers, are dressed for a party. They sit silently waiting for the responding welcome.

"Welcome, yes, welcome!" Father's voice booms like a drum. "We are honored by your coming to our humble village. You will bring cheer to us all. Come ashore, come ashore!" Father is dressed in his finest white mountain goat robe. Red, brown, and black geometric patterns trim its edges. The robe, woven by Mother, had been a gift to Grandfather and then was passed down to Father.

Joining him are other relatives, all looking very regal as they line the beach. Soon, the drums begin to beat rapidly and a chorus of voices sings the ancestral welcoming song. The canoes seem to float ashore on the music. People rush to lift the guests onto the beach. The party is about to begin!

9

The villagers gather at Father's house. Wonderful smells of dinner excite everyone as salmon and seal, seaweed and salmon egg soup, baked camas and clover roots, soapberry foam, and the finest eulachon fish oil are all served. After everyone has eaten, leaders from the village give welcoming speeches to the guests from up-river. Uncle responds by presenting gifts of food they have brought with them. There are many baskets and boxes filled with huckleberries and blueberries, smoked bear and deer meat, and fresh elk and mountain goat meat.

It is late into the night when Father and Mother bring

out their gifts. Brother helps present special gifts for all the visitors. He gives blankets and robes that Mother and Auntie have woven. There are also bone pendants and canoe paddles that Father and Brother have carved. Finally, Brother presents a basket and his newly carved spindle whorl to Uncle's wife. With a smile of joy, she pulls ball after ball of Sulsuliya's spun yarn out of the basket.

With the guests now gone, Mother sits in the silent house weaving at her loom. Sulsuliya watches Auntie spinning. Someday she will spin like her with a large spindle whorl.

"Sulsuliya," calls Grandmother. "Come and sit beside me."

As she kneels down beside Grandmother, she notices a bulging cedar mat package by her feet and a large old spindle whorl in Grandmother's hands. Sulsuliya's heart begins to race.

"I have something important to say," Grandmother begins. "You have greatly pleased all the members of our house. Your gift to Uncle's wife of finely spun wool shows how you have lived up to your adult name. It is a name to which you bring honor."

Slowly, Grandmother loosens the cedar bark strings that hold the package together. Sulsuliya gasps as out tumbles mountain goat wool. "Uncle left a special gift for you to spin," Grandmother whispers. Little Sister climbs up to see. "Oh, Sulsuliya, how lucky!" she exclaims.

"And now I am getting too old," Grandmother continues. "I cannot spin with this large spindle whorl as I once did. You will spin the mountain goat wool with it now."

"Grandmother," asks Little Sister, "what is the animal carved on the whorl?"

Grandmother gently strokes Little Sister's long black hair. "Tell me, Granddaughter, what do you think it might be?"

"It's a bird flying," Little Sister guesses. "But, Grandmother, I also see the head of a fish. I know, I know! It's an eagle with a salmon in its belly." Grandmother chuckles. "The image in the whorl is what you see, what you understand, and what you experience."

Sulsuliya and Grandmother smile at one another. Sulsuliya holds back tears of joy as Grandmother hands her the large old spindle whorl. "Your great-great-Grandfather carved it for me when I came of age and was given my adult name," said Grandmother. "Now you will spin with it until someday, as a grandmother, you too will hand it down."

TAKE WINGS AND FLY!

Grandmother's large spindle whorl might have looked like this whorl, which is currently at the Smithsonian Institution, a museum in Washington, D.C. Whorls like this one were carved and used by Central Coast Salish people.

The bird image on this whorl was made by a Central Coast Salish carver. He created the outline of the bird, then carved away the area around the bird. This recessed area surrounding the bird becomes negative surface.

If the space around the bird is negative, what part of the whorl is positive surface?

Answer: The raised surface of the bird

14

CUT

PASTE

CUT

EXPLORE THE IMPORTANCE OF SPACE

The carver was very clever in making this bird look as if it were flying. It is an illusion created by at least four clues carved into the bird, and two clues in the area around the bird. Remember, this area around the bird is called negative space. Discover the illusion of flight!

YOU NEED:

whorl on page 14

pencil

thick colored marker

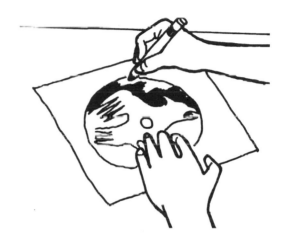

DIRECTIONS:

1. Color the negative space around the bird.

2. Can you find four things the carver did to make the bird look like it is flying?

Clue 1 _____ Clue 2 _____

Clue 3 _____ Clue 4 _____

3. Look at the colored area between the bird and the edge of the whorl. Can you find two clues here that give the illusion of flight? (Hint: Look for the least and most amounts of space.)

Clue 5 _____ Clue 6 _____

Answers:
1. Wing uplifted
2. Tail turned up
3. Foot pulled up
4. Designs going in same direction to look windswept
5. Least space at beak, as bird flies off whorl
6. Most space under the bird, lifting it into air

INSIDE SCOOP

Inside the bird, special shapes are scooped out. These cuts, carved as shown here, become recessed or negative surface.

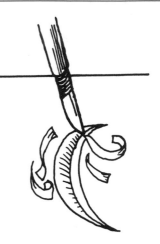

Try your skill at forming this basic cut of Central Coast Salish art by tracing over the dotted lines below. Which part is the base? Which part is the bulge?

YOU NEED:

pencil

thick marker

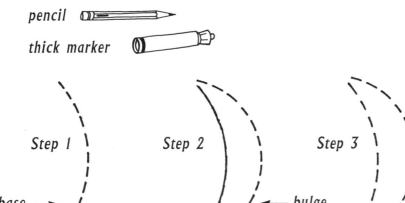

Step 1

base →

Step 2

← *bulge*

Step 3

What does this shape look like?_____

Draw a few
more cuts in
this space.

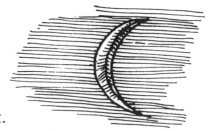

Today Central Coast Salish artists call this cut a crescent.

Below is a second cut. Draw this cut by tracing over the dotted lines in each step.

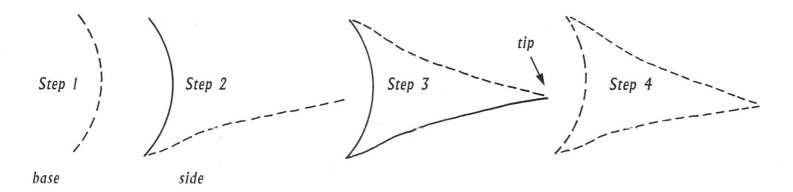

Step 1

base

Step 2

side

Step 3

tip

Step 4

What does this shape look like? _____

Which part is the tip?   The base?

Draw a few more of these on your own.

This cut is called a wedge. Maybe you've seen a wedge used to split wood. A maul or heavy hammer drives the wedge deep into the wood.

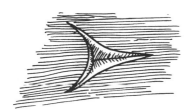

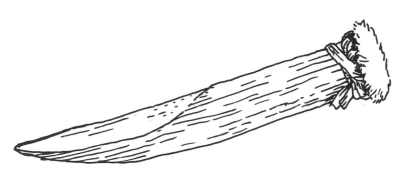

The illustration here shows a traditional Coast Salish wedge used for splitting wood, like the cedar planks on page 7.

REPEATING PATTERNS

As crescents and wedges are carved into the raised (or positive) surface of an image, repeating patterns are created. There are many combinations.

Because these shapes cut away the positive surface, they are considered negative surface.

Using the patterns below to get you started, draw more crescents and wedges, showing how you would continue the pattern.

YOU NEED:

pencil

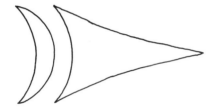

Pattern #1

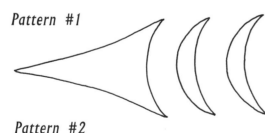

Pattern #2

Point to the tips of the wedges and the bulges of the crescents. Which direction do they seem to go? An illusion of movement has been created. Draw an arrow next to each pattern pointing in the direction it is moving.

SWIMMING SALMON

Central Coast Salish artists carve patterns of crescents and wedges into the raised (positive) surface of fish, to show the illusion of the body parts and movement. Let's see what illusions you can find.

YOU NEED:

marker

pencil

scissors

Look at the circle, or what might be the eye of the fish. Is it really the eye or the pupil of the fish's eye? Find out by coloring a ring around the circle, the positive surface of the eye. Use the wedges to help define the edge of this ring.

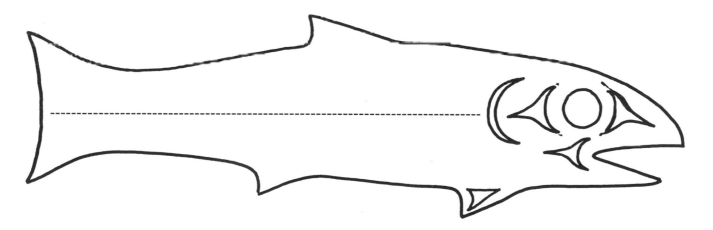

Can you see an illusion of lips created by a third wedge? Color the lips!
Now, finish coloring in all the positive surface of the fish.

DIRECTIONS:

1. Color the positive surface of the fish below.

2. Cut out the fish and fold it in half along the dotted line.

3. Along the folded edge draw a pattern of half crescents and half wedges.

4. With the fish still folded, cut out the half crescents and half wedges you drew.

5. Unfold the fish.

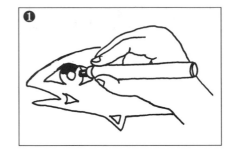

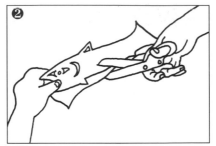

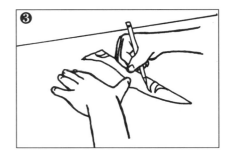

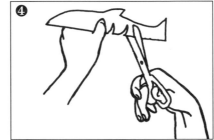

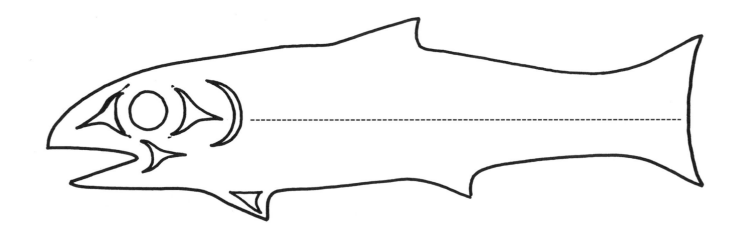

Are the crescents and wedges even (symmetrical) on both sides of the fish? Why?
Think up ways to display your swimming salmon.

ANIMAL IN THE ROUND

This is part of a spindle whorl now at the Smithsonian Institution. Finish the animal shape on this whorl.

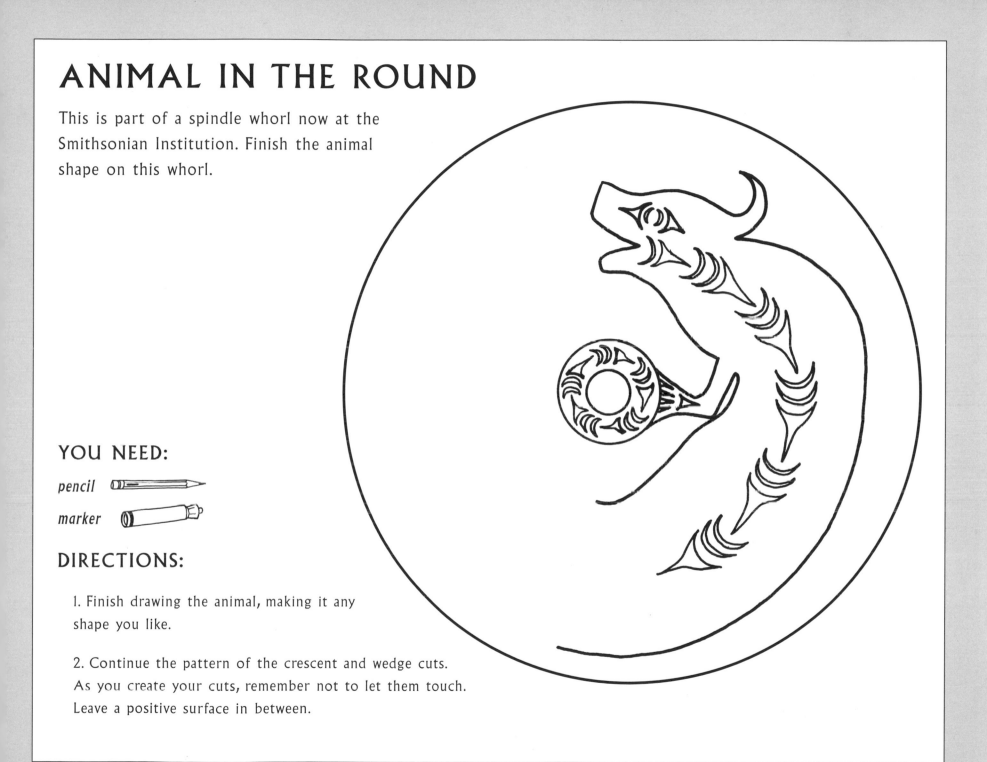

YOU NEED:

pencil

marker

DIRECTIONS:

1. Finish drawing the animal, making it any shape you like.

2. Continue the pattern of the crescent and wedge cuts. As you create your cuts, remember not to let them touch. Leave a positive surface in between.

OPTICAL ILLUSIONS

This is how the original artist carved the spindle whorl. Perhaps your animal's body is different. But, more than likely, you continued the same pattern of crescents and wedges. Discover the optical illusion the carver created with positive and negative.

YOU NEED:

colored marker

your eyes

DIRECTIONS:

1. Color the positive surface of the animal's body. Leave all negative cuts white.

2. Discover the optical illusion by holding the whorl eight inches away from your eyes. Stare at one spot between the tip of a wedge and the base of a crescent.

3. Count to 20 and immediately shut your eyes to see the optical illusion.

4. Which image is stronger—the positive body surface or the negative cuts?

THE SPLITTING WEDGE

Central Coast Salish artists use one other cut in their relief carving. It looks like a wedge splitting something open.

Try your skill at splitting with a wedge.

YOU NEED:

pencil

thick marker

DIRECTIONS:

1. Draw this new cut by tracing over the dotted lines.

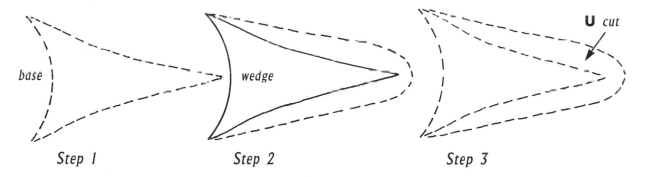

base

wedge

U *cut*

Step 1   *Step 2*   *Step 3*

2. What does the final drawing look like?_____ This cut is called a "split **U**."

3. Try drawing several split **U** cuts on your own.

POSITIVE AND NEGATIVE: COMPLEMENTARY PATTERNS

Using the split **U**, continue the existing patterns on the animal below.

YOU NEED:

pencil

markers

DIRECTIONS:

Using different colored markers for the different cuts and for the positive surface, color the animal.

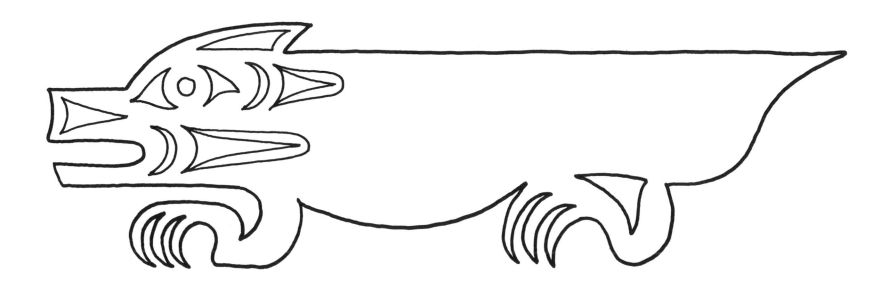

WHAT IS MOTIONLESS BUT MOVES?

Discover what makes this traditional whorl an eye dazzler.
This whorl is also housed at the Smithsonian
Institution.

YOU NEED:

dark marker

pencil

a partner

DIRECTIONS:

1. Color the positive surface of the animal. Do not
color inside the crescents, wedges, or split **U**'s.

2. When finished, ask a partner to watch your eyes and
record which direction your eyes move as you look at the image:

    circular   *back and forth*   *wavy/zigzag*

3. What creates the eye-dazzling movement within the animal?

*Answer: The reversed patterns of **U**'s and crescents*

TWO CONTEMPORARY WHORL DESIGNS

Roger Fernandes, a Coast Salish artist, carved this design on a linoleum block and then made a print from it. He calls it "Eagles and Salmon." Can you see the eagles and the salmon? Can you also find the illusion of a face?

Susan Point, a Central Coast Salish artist, titled this print "Swanisit Brings Salmon II." Swanisit was an ancestor who brought salmon to the Coast Salish people. Susan designed her print in the shape of a whorl. What images do you see in this whorl?

ANIMAL IMPRESSIONS

Roger Fernandes and Susan Point used the positive and negative surfaces in their whorl designs to print the image on paper. Try drawing and printing your own animal design.

YOU NEED:

paper

pencil

scratch-foam (4" x 6") or foam meat tray (use smooth side)

table knife

all-purpose glue

foam core (8½" x 11")

newspaper for table covering

tempura paint

your finger or an art roller

DIRECTIONS:

1. On paper, draw the outline of any animal you want. Then draw crescents ⟩, wedges ▷, and split **U**'s ▷, on the body of the animal, creating your own design pattern.

2. Lay the paper on the foam. Trace the outline of your animal and design, pressing hard enough to push into the foam.

3. With a table knife press the inside of ⟩, ▷, and ▷ into the foam.

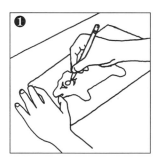

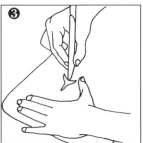

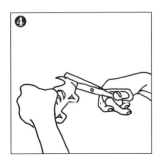

4. Cut out the animal outline from the foam.

5. Turn the animal over, apply glue to the underside, and press it to the foam core.

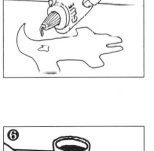

6. When the glue is dry, apply paint to the positive, or raised, surface of the animal only!

7. While the paint is still wet, carefully lay paper over the inked design. Rub with your hands or an art roller, while holding the paper firmly in place.

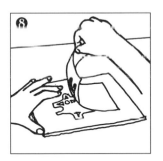

8. Pull the paper off slowly and let it dry.

MAKE A WHORL

YOU NEED:

color insert of whorl

pencil

poster board or file folders

scissors

all-purpose glue

paper clips

compass

DIRECTIONS:

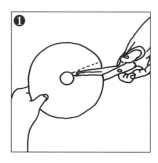

1. Cut out the whorl from the insert of this book. Trace the outline of the cut-out whorl on the poster board.

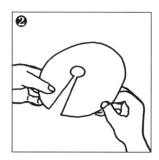

2. Bend the colored whorl so its ends overlap. The image should be convex, or bending outward.

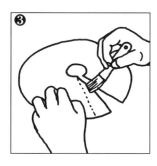

3. Put glue on the white pie-shaped area.

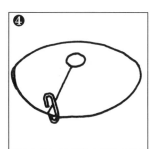

4. Slide it under the colored surface and fasten with a paper clip. Let it dry.

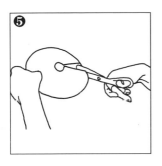

5. Cut out the whorl from the poster board.

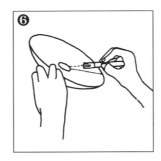

6. Bend the poster board whorl (so that its ends overlap) and put glue on the pie area. Slide it under the other side and use a paper clip to fasten the ends together. Let dry.

7. Glue the plain poster board whorl to the back, or concave, side of the colored whorl.

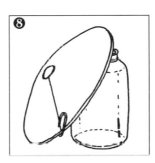

8. Fasten the two whorls together with paper clips and let dry.

While you let your new whorl dry, make the shaft that goes through the center hole. (See the next page.)

ROLL THE SHAFT

YOU NEED:

butcher paper (18" x 24")

hard surface to roll on

scotch tape

paper whorl (see pages 30–31)

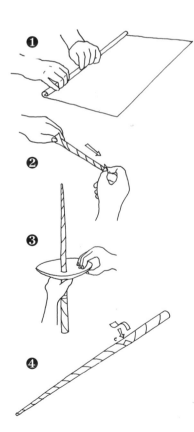

❶

❷

❸

❹

DIRECTIONS:

1. Fold a $^{1}/_{8}$" crease along the long edge of the paper. Roll the paper tightly!

2. Tightly twist one end of the roll to make a cone shape. Now gently pull the exposed tip of paper out on the tight end.

3. Slip the design side of whorl first down the narrow end of the rolled shaft to about 10" from the thick end. Loosen the thick end to enlarge it so that it fits tightly.

4. Remove the whorl and tape the paper's exposed edges. Tuck in loose paper at the large end, and replace the whorl.

For directions on how to spin wool on your spindle, see pages 36-38 in the Adult Teaching Section.

ADULT TEACHING GUIDE

The Spindle Whorl is the fourth book in a four-part series on Northwest Coast Indian art. It is preceded by *The Bentwood Box, The Button Blanket,* and *The Cedar Plank Mask.* This book is designed for school-age children from 3rd to 6th grades; younger students will especially enjoy the spinning!

Each book represents a different style of art developed by Native peoples along the Northwest Coast. This fourth book, *The Spindle Whorl,* discusses the Central Coast Salish art style, as it is often represented by carvings on the whorl of a spindle. The spindle was used all along the Northwest Coast, but the only whorls with decorative carving were those of the Central Coast Salish, who lived along the rivers and inland waters of what is today northwest Washington and southwest British Columbia.

INTRODUCTION TO ADULT MATERIAL

If you are a teacher, scout leader, or an adult looking for group activities for children, these pages were written just for you. Note that there is no mention of transparencies here; however, the children's activity pages may be duplicated for group use.

Spinning and weaving were—and are today—a part of Native people's lives all up and down the Northwest Coast. Involvement in both activities helps nurture and sustain traditional values in Native life.

For more information about Central Coast Salish people and their art, the following select reference materials will be very helpful.

SELECT BIBLIOGRAPHY

Carlson, Roy L. ed. *Indian Art Traditions of the Northwest Coast.* Burnaby, B.C.: Archaeology Press, 1976.

Crockford, Susan J. *Osteometry of Makah and Coast Salish Dogs.* Burnaby, B.C.: Archaeology Press, 1997.

Feder, Norman. "Incised Relief Carving of the Halkomelem and Straits Salish." *American Indian Art Magazine* (Spring 1983).

Gunther, Erna. *Indian Life on the Northwest Coast of North America.* Chicago: University of Chicago Press, 1972.

Gustafson, Paula. *Salish Weaving.* Vancouver, B.C.: Douglas and McIntyre, Ltd.; Seattle: University of Washington Press, 1980.

Halliday, Jan and Gail Chehak. *Native Peoples of the Northwest: A Traveler's Guide to Land, Art and Culture.* Seattle: Sasquatch Books, 1996.

Hill-Tout, Charles. *The Salish People.* vols. 1-5, ed. Ralph Maud. Vancouver, B.C.: Talonbooks, 1978.

Holm, Bill. *Spirit and Ancestor.* Seattle: Burke Museum; Vancouver, B.C.: Douglas and McIntyre, Ltd., 1987.

Johnson, Elizabeth L. and Kathryn Bernick. *Hands of Our Ancestors, The Revival of Salish ,Weaving at Musqueam.* Museum Note No. 16. Vancouver, B.C.: University of British Columbia Museum of Anthropology, 1986.

Kew, J.E. Michael. *Sculpture and Engraving of the Central Coast Salish Indians.* Museum Note No. 9. Vancouver, B.C.: University of British Columbia Museum of Anthropology, 1970.

Macnair, Peter L., Alan L. Hoover, and Kevin Neary. *The Legacy.* Victoria, B.C.: British Columbia Provincial Museum, 1980.

Suttles, Wayne. *Coast Salish Essays.* Vancouver, B.C.: Talonbooks, 1987.

CENTRAL COAST SALISH PEOPLES

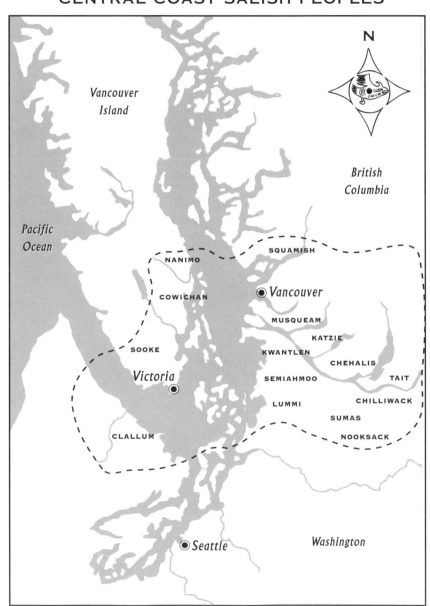

MORE ABOUT THE STORY

In studying other cultures, the focus is often on traditional values and practices because they are so different from what we know today. Contemporary culture is sometimes ignored and, thus, not recognized by those being educated. All cultures change through time, a fact that we tend to forget. In your studies of Native American cultures, seek to also include how those people live today. Two other books in this series, *The Button Blanket* and *The Cedar Plank Mask*, feature simple stories about contemporary Indian children that will enhance your studies.

Cultural change through time is an important concept that affects us all, our own culture being in constant flux. It can be difficult for people living in mainstream society to even recognize that they have a specific culture. To strengthen the notion that all cultures change through time, include a parallel study where each child researches his or her own culture and how it has changed over time.

Today, Indian children are as modern as any other kids. They wear jeans and the latest fad in clothing, play soccer and basketball, and read books that inspire their thoughts and aspirations. And yet, Indian children inherit a culture that is thousands of years old. While these values and practices have changed through time, there is a continuum that links them to their past—just as every child is linked to some kind of distant past.

STAGES OF LIFE—THE STORY

This story uses a number of female characters to portray the potential of a Central Coast Salish woman's life before the coming of Euro-Americans in the 1700s. The central character Sulsuliya is a young woman, about 13 to 15 years of age, from a well-to-do family. Her family has been able to afford the expense of a naming celebration, in which ancestral names are passed on to both her brother and herself.

She has proven herself as a hard and conscientious worker, particularly as a fine spinner. And by this time, she probably has received a guardian spirit helper and spiritual vision, which are important elements in becoming an adult. She probably has also had her first menses and received training in the proper etiquette of an eligible woman.

The younger sister allows us to see how Sulsuliya might have been as a young girl: emotionally expressive, curious, playful, yet learning how to attend to tasks at the side of the older women. One such task is helping with the baby.

Typical of babies from the Central Coast Salish upper class, this baby is cradled in a basket, her head gently bound with cedar bark to slope the forehead. Sulsuliya was also cradled in this way, as were all others, giving her face a broad appearance. This was not only a sign of beauty but also a sign of wealth for both men and women.

Older, though not by much, is Uncle's new wife. We see only a glimpse of her, yet her presence suggests the next step in Sulsuliya's life. She wears wool blankets indicating that she is also from an upper class family. She is from another village, increasing the economic diversity and status for both sets of parents-in-law.

At the time of this story, Sulsuliya's parents have already made arrangements for her future husband. While we might see arranged marriages in a negative light, the knowledge that her parents are helping in the preparation of her adult life gives Sulsuliya the freedom to concentrate on achievement in spinning and other abilities.

Sulsuliya's mother and aunt represent the next stage in a woman's life. When Mother married, she moved to her husband's house on the coast, leaving her own village up-river. She has children, is a highly accomplished weaver, and acts as a full partner in the family economic affairs. This is demonstrated by the party, a time of exchanging food and gifts between the in-laws. While not a true potlatch, such as a naming ceremony, this type of party is important to both Father and Mother's families in maintaining status and economic stability for the future of their children.

Finally at the end of the story, Grandmother, representing the last stage of a Central Coast Salish woman's life, gives a gift of an heirloom to Sulsuliya and a gift of wisdom to Little Sister. While she will continue to carry on her daily tasks in her extended family's home as long as she can, her utmost concern now lies in guiding her grandchildren's proper behavior, maintaining their status, encouraging their achievements, and teaching them family lineage and spiritual knowledge.

DOGS, MOUNTAIN GOATS, AND WOOL

Creating a story that takes place before the coming of Euro-Americans requires the blending of scant and sometimes conflicting references derived from oral and written literature. However, it is clear from ethnographic and archaeological accounts that the special "wool dog" was a small- to medium-size, curly tail dog, bred exclusively for its woolly fur.

While an exact date for the origin of wool dogs is not yet known, the first archaeological evidence of a domesticated breed thought to be the small animals dates back 3,000 years. These dogs were kept isolated from other dogs so that interbreeding would not occur. The wool dogs were always attended by women and were possibly the property of women. They were fed special diets, sometimes even lived in the homes, and were sheared like sheep for the highly prized commodity of their fur, or wool.

By the 1800s, with the vast influx of Euro-American culture and the ensuing disruption of traditional Indian life, the wool dog had disappeared. Today what remains of this old Central Coast Salish wool dog tradition are the stories, the yarn and the blankets, the spinning and

weaving implements, and the residue of white clay used for cleaning the wool.

The use of mountain goat wool lasted longer. The goat lived in the Cascade and Coastal mountains and its wool could be easily gathered from the low branches of wild huckleberry bushes growing there.

The coat of the mountain goat is different from that of the dog. While the wool dog had only one type of hair, the mountain goat's coat consisted of long, coarse guard hairs and short, thick soft hair. Women pulled out as many long guard hairs as possible, leaving the rest to be spun.

The wool, whether from dogs or mountain goats, needed to be cleaned. The primary ingredient for this task was white clay, or diatomaceous earth. This substance is from ancient deposits of the diatom's siliceous skeleton; its three-dimensional skeleton effectively traps particles. Today, crushed diatoms are used as cleaning filters for rocket fuel, swimming pool filters, and even as a bug retardant in gardens. The Central

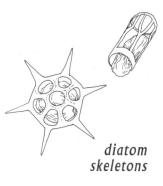

diatom skeletons

Coast Salish people discovered and used the excellent cleaning qualities of diatomaceous earth to "dry clean" their wool.

The smaller Central Coast Salish spindles (such as the one on page 1) were used for spinning fine threads of dog and mountain goat wool, as well as stinging nettles and Indian hemp to make twine for nets. The larger whorls, with diameters up to 8 inches, were used for spinning thick yarns and for twisting two yarns together, a process called plying.

The advantage of plied yarn is that it is much stronger then single strands of yarn, with the twist of the ply running opposite to the twist of the original spin. The two yarns were drawn through an elevated tension ring and down to the whorl, which the spinner balanced upright on the palm of her hand.

SPINNING WITH YOUR SPINDLE

While you may never have spun wool, take the time to do this activity. You cannot imagine how rewarding it will be for you and your children or students. Don't be too surprised when you find out that many children do not know that clothing is made from threads and yarns!

There are several steps that you must do to make this activity successful. Locate a wool shop where you can buy the needed supplies.

You need (for each child):
1 oz of carded wool (Coopworth wool works best)
1/2 oz of uncarded wool
a sharp pair of scissors
scraps of yarn, twine, and rope

1. Make the paper spindle whorl (instructions are on pages 30-32) before you begin the activities on Central Coast Salish art. (If you are a wood worker, you may want to make a spindle

from a wooden dowel and a flat whorl from plywood. Glue the whorl in place so that it will not slip.)

2. On your own, follow the instructions below to learn how to spin. Then demonstrate spinning while the children are doing the art activities. (Use a stool for better viewing.) This will give the children the advantage of knowing what the spindle whorl is and how it works. You will also be reinforcing the skill of observation.

3. Discuss with them the traditional ways Northwest Coast Indian children and apprentices learned from masters. First children and apprentices observed for a long time without questions. Watching every movement and step of the process, they learned to imitate the actions of the skilled person and, when alone, they would practice. Finally, when their efforts were successful, they worked alongside the skilled person.

BACKGROUND INFORMATION

Spinning wool does not require a spindle, shaft, or whorl. In fact a lot of spinning was—and still is—done by twisting wool or a combination of wool and yellow cedar bark on a person's thigh. The mechanical advantage of the spindle whorl is that the weight of the whorl and its inertia reduces the effort of the hand.

Spindle whorls vary in sizes up and down the Northwest Coast. The whorls made by the northern tribes are approximately 2½ inches to 3 inches in diameter, sometimes concave but also flat. The accompanying spindle shafts average about 16 inches in length. None of these whorls are carved with designs.

Whorls of the more southern tribes—the Central Coast Salish, Makah, and Nootka—vary widely, ranging from about 3 inches to 12 inches in diameter. Adornment is limited to the larger whorls, though many of those are also plain. The shafts for the large whorls are up to 4 feet long.

As Central Coast Salish women spun mountain goat or dog wool, additional substances were sometimes added to extend the materials being spun. Fluff from cattail heads or fireweed, as well as duck down, were added to supplement the wool and its insulating value.

Today only a few people use spindles. Most home spinning is done on a mechanized spinner, fashioned from an old sewing machine and driven by a foot pedal.

ACTIVITIES

Wool. What is it?

1. Divide the uncarded wool among the children. Allow time for them to play with the wool.

2. Look at the wool under a magnifying lens or microscope.

3. Ask them what would happen if we washed the wool, or pulled the wool out as far as we could? The children will have lots of ideas.

UNWINDING YARN, TWINE, AND ROPE

1. Have the children handle several samples of scrap yarn, twine, and rope. Ask them to take their sample apart by untwisting it.

2. With the samples in front of them, discuss what they have observed.

3. Now have them try to twist the samples back together.

MAKING A ROVING FROM WOOL

The spindle whorl should be completed before beginning this step. Instructions for making the spindle whorl are on pages 30-32.

1. Unroll the carded wool and separate out a section of fibers, approximately 12" x 1" x 1/4".

2. Gently pull on the ends of the fibers, so that you lengthen but thin the entire bunch to

approximately 24" x 1/2" x 1/2". Don't over-pull or the fibers will fall apart.

3. Lay the bunch of fibers on the top of your thigh and roll them down your thigh. What you have just made is called a roving. This process of rolling helps make the fibers more compact and hold together better.

ROLLING THE SHAFT

1. Lay the spindle across the top of your lap. If you are right handed, the thick end of the spindle should rest on your right thigh. Left-handed people should do the opposite.

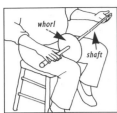

2. Make sure that your legs are spread apart enough so that the whorl fits between them. Identify the parts of the spindle: shaft and whorl.

3. Lightly place your right hand, palm down, on the base of the spindle, which is resting on your right thigh.

4. With open palm, use your left hand to gently lift the small end of the shaft.

5. With your right palm, lightly press the shaft and gently roll it down your right thigh. Keep your palm on the shaft at all times.

6. While you are rolling with your right hand, your left hand cups and steadies the tip of the shaft but does not move.

7. Once the base of the shaft reaches the end of your thigh, lift it up and draw it back to the top of your right thigh with your right hand.

8. Practice this rolling until you feel comfortable and in control of the spindle whorl.

ATTACHING THE ROVING TO THE SPINDLE

1. Remove the whorl so that you can insert the end of the roving into the center hole.

2. With the roving inside the center hole of the

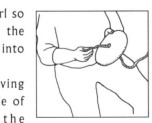

whorl, gently pull the whorl down the shaft until it fits snugly and the roving is tightly secured.

SPINNING YARN

1. Lay the spindle back on your lap.

2. With your left hand pick up the roving between your thumb and index finger, pinching it tightly.

3. Rest the small end of the shaft in your left palm. Cup your hand to secure the tip.

4. Place your right hand on the base of the shaft, which is resting on your right thigh, and roll the shaft down your leg. This twists, or spins, the roving into yarn.

5. While spinning, keep the roving tightly pinched between your thumb and finger and hold it straight out from the end of the shaft.

6. Continue this spinning action while you tightly pinch the roving.

7. Stop the spinning action and look at the twists that have gathered in front of your left thumb and index finger.

8. Slowly and gently loosen your pinch, without letting go of the roving, and slide your thumb and index finger away from you and up the roving.

9. Watch the twists travel up the roving. When they stop, apply your pinch once more.

WRAPPING THE YARN AROUND THE SHAFT

When the yarn becomes too long to continue spinning, you are ready to ball the yarn around the spindle.

1. With your hands, yarn, and spindle in the spinning position, use your left hand to pull the

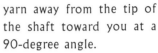

yarn away from the tip of the shaft toward you at a 90-degree angle.

2. With your right hand, lift the spindle and hold it

upright. Then turn the shaft. As you do this, the yarn will wrap around the shaft, balling up in the dish of your whorl.

3. Keep turning the shaft until your left hand meets the tip of the shaft. You are ready to begin spinning again.

ADDING A NEW ROVING

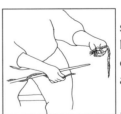

1. When you've finished spinning the first roving, leave the ball of yarn in the dish of the whorl and make a new roving.

2. Pinch the new roving to the end of the newly spun yarn.

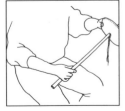

3. Continue spinning, allowing the twists to build up by your pinched fingers.

4. Loosen and slide your finger and thumb up the roving, allowing the twists to continue up the new yarn.

5. Continue spinning, adding new roving and winding the yarn around the shaft.

6. If at any time you wish to stop spinning, wind all the yarn around the shaft. The yarn fibers will catch one another and hold it all in place.

7. To remove the yarn from the shaft, simply slip the wrapped yarn ball off the shaft and store in a sack or basket.

INTRODUCTION TO CENTRAL COAST SALISH ART

The earliest archaeological findings of Central Coast Salish art (decorated stone, bone, and antler fragments) date to 3,600 years ago. These artifacts demonstrate the antiquity of an art form that has become more highly stylized in modern times. About 2,500 years ago, Central Coast Salish artists began to use crescents, **U** forms, circles, ovals, and wedge-shaped gouges to

pin

delineate the various parts of the animals they carved. These design elements are demonstrated on the three artifacts illustrated here: a pin, a brow band fragment, and a slotted antler cylinder.

brow band

cylinder

A word should be interjected here about the names by which these cuts and forms are identified in this book: the crescent, wedge, split **U**, and **U** cut. The traditional names for these cuts and forms no longer exist, so to enable communication, a set vocabulary has been established by artists and scholars. As your children indicate what the cuts look like to them, let them know that their names are just as valid as the names used today.

It was not until the 1800s that complete spindle whorls were discovered. Perhaps this was due to poor preservation or to the minimal number of Native sites that had been excavated. In any case, wooden whorls, usually made from maple, were discovered more often than whorls made from stone or bone. Most of the wooden whorls are plain, but those that are carved reveal a wide range of techniques suggesting that both amateurs and highly skilled artisans decorated the whorls.

The whorls were never painted. But today, as whorl designs are printed on paper (like the colored whorl in this book) artists use paint to portray the traditional carvings on the whorl.

The Central Coast Salish peoples were—and still are—concerned with the privacy of personal designs. This is very different from the northern Northwest Coast Indians who publicly display their family or clan designs in the form of crests. Among the Central Coast Salish peoples, depictions, if any, are limited to symbolic designs or generic representations of fish, birds, reptiles, and mammals (including humans).

Objects that were most often decorated were spinning and weaving implements, such as the spindle whorl, as well as rattles, masks, and house poles. Combs, like

the one shown below (circa 1800), were not only used as personal objects but may also have been used to comb the wool dogs.

It is thought that spindle whorls were decorated because of their importance in the cleansing process that wool went through as it was transformed into yarn and, finally, into blankets, a major source of wealth.

To introduce the story and the activities, use the resource books listed in the bibliography (page 34) to show other whorls, as well as the processes of spinning and weaving.

INTRODUCTORY ACTIVITIES

1. The first activity on pages 14 and 15, the flying bird, is a general exercise to show how background is carved away, leaving a raised surface, or positive image, and a recessed, or negative, surface. Ask the children to identify the positive and negative surfaces. This style of carving is called relief.

2. Experiment with negative and positive surfaces by using the whorl design on page 14. Cut away the negative surface that surrounds the bird image. Glue the image onto a disk (or whorl) made of dark paper. This will increase the awareness of the negative surface that surrounds the positive image of the bird.

3. Activities on pages 16 and 17 introduce the symmetrical shallow cuts on the surface of the raised positive image. These cuts are negative surfaces within the relief carving. They help define the positive body parts, movement, and spiritual presence within the body of the image. Here, the children are asked to color with a marker the positive surface that surrounds the negative crescent- and wedge-shaped cuts. Note that some children will simply outline the cuts, while others will color a larger area around them. Both are acceptable.

4. While the wedge cut on page  17 is rather short and wide, wedge cuts also can be long and narrow. Identify the long, pointed wedges on pages 14 and 26, and have the children draw a few examples.

5. Page 18 emphasizes patterns made by crescents and wedges. Use this exercise to focus on the positive surfaces the children created *between* the cuts. Have them use a marker to color the area that surrounds one pattern of cuts; this is the positive surface between the crescents and wedges. Does this positive surface have a pattern? (The answer may vary depending on how uniform the cut shapes are.) If so, what is that pattern? (Again, answers may vary, but the children should see that the positive surface between the cuts mimics the actual form of the cut.) Where is this positive pattern clearly defined? (Answer: between the edges of the cut, or negative surface.) Finally, ask the children what they have determined about the relationship between positive surfaces and negative cuts. (One answer might be that one does not exist without the other.)

6. Following the fish activity on pages 19-20, return to the question of negative and positive surfaces. What happens to the positive surface not precisely defined by negative cuts? (Answer: the positive surface not found between the cuts represents the positive surface of the whole fish.)

7. For additional fun, have the children create different ways to display their fish!

ANIMAL IN THE ROUND

Activity

1. Before introducing the activities on pages 21 and 22, have the children draw a native animal with crescents and wedges defining body parts and movement—their own Central Coast Salish design!

2. The image on page 22 is an optical illusion. Some children will see the positive surface in the animal without coloring it. Others will need to color the surface before their eyes and mind can pay attention to the positive image of the animal. Have them concentrate on the positive space between the tip of a wedge and the base of a crescent. In doing so, some children will see the positive surface more clearly than the negative, or vice versa. (Be sure to have them relax their eyes between each viewing attempt.)

3. Discuss what animal is represented on this whorl (page 22). Central Coast Salish people call this image a fisher. The fisher is a member of the Martin family and is smaller and darker than a weasel.

4. Try the same optical activity from above with the whorl design on page 27.

THE SPLITTING WEDGE

A third cut used on some whorls is a "**U** cut" carved around a wedge. The combination of the wedge and **U** cut is called a "split **U**." The visual effect created by the split **U** is stimulating and might be interpreted as quick movements or intense energy.

Activity

1. Review the way wedges are made on page 17 before introducing the split **U**'s on page 23. After completing page 23, have the children look for split **U**'s in all of the whorls. Notice the different sizes that exist as well as the different patterns. Discuss the visual impact that occurs in each whorl.

2. Using the whorl on page 14, ask the children to trace with their fingers the positive surface between a split **U** and a crescent, following along the sides of the split **U**. What figure or shape is it that they trace? (Answer: a crescent or a **U** cut.) This positive surface alongside the crescent and split **U** is called a "**U** form."

3. Using a copy of the whorl on page 21, have the children create a pattern that uses split **U**'s and crescents. Ask the children to describe what change the split **U**'s make in their perception of the image.

ANIMAL IMPRESSIONS

Central Coast Salish carved objects were meant as designs in themselves. But because the carving was done as a relief, it is possible to use this type of art to make prints or impressions on paper. The following activity explores relief carving by printing each child's own creative image.

While the materials listed on page 28 can be used, the following directions are written for students who can handle Exacto blades. You may also want to locate a local sign supply store that does sandblasting and handles *Signblast Tape* or *Sandblast Mask*. These products have a sticky surface sandwiched between a latex and plastic surface. The advantage of this is simplicity. The latex can be drawn on and cut, and the plastic peeled away so that the sticky surface can be adhered to a foam core base.

Activity

1. Have the children create an image with crescent, wedge, and split **U** shapes. They can then transfer their creation onto the latex side of the Signblast Tape, either by redrawing it or tracing it with carbon.

2. Using scissors, cut out the image.

3. After centering the image on a piece of foam core, remove the plastic backing of the image and press it onto the foam core.

4. Using a blade or razor knife, cut around the interior shapes and pull them away. The result is a relief carving of the image.

5. With extra Signblast Tape, make a frame around the foam core's outer edge. This provides an outer edge surface for the roller when you apply the paint.

6. If you are using an art roller to apply paint, pour a small amount of paint in the bottom of a shallow rectangular pan. Roll excess paint on the edge of the pan.

7. For a variation, try making paint from salmon eggs as was done long ago. Instructions are in *The Bentwood Box*. (Note: this paint is an oil base paint and is difficult to clean with water. You may want paint thinner or turpentine handy in case a spill occurs.)

DESIGN YOUR OWN WHORL

Using pages 30 and 31, create an original design on a whorl. This activity will challenge students but can be quite rewarding. If they have never worked with a compass, allow time for children to explore the instrument's use and make circles.

You need:

compass with pencil
ruler
2 colored pencils, a dark and light of
  same color
poster board

Directions:
Drawing the Whorl

1. Review the steps for making a whorl on pages 30 and 31.

2. Hand out the compasses and poster board. Have students set each compass at 3 1/2" for the radius of the whorl.

3. Draw a circle by placing the compass's point in the center of the desired space. Turn the compass so the pencil outlines a circle. This is the outer edge of the spindle whorl.

4. Next, children will set each compass at 1/4", center the compass point in the first large circle, and draw the center hole in the whorl in the same way. The center hole is for the shaft of the spindle.

5. With a ruler, draw a solid line from the center hole to the outer edge of the whorl; this is the radius. Draw a second radius line, beginning 1/8" away from the first radius on the center hole, but make this second line dotted.

6. Now have children cut out the whorl, cutting along the outer edge. Then cut along the solid radius line to the center. Finally, cut out the center circle. Leave the dotted radius line in tact.

Designing the Whorl

1. The design on the newly cut whorl is up to each student's imagination.

2. Use two colored pencils, a dark and a light of the same color, which will give the feeling of a carved relief and an illusion of depth. The darker color is best for the negative, or cut, surface.

Assembling the Whorl

1. With compass and poster board, have students make a second whorl, following the instructions above. (This whorl will have no art design as it will hold the spun wool.)

2. Using the directions on pages 30 and 31, construct complete whorls from the 2 the children have cut out here. When the 2 halves are together, refer to page 32 on how to assemble a spindle shaft.

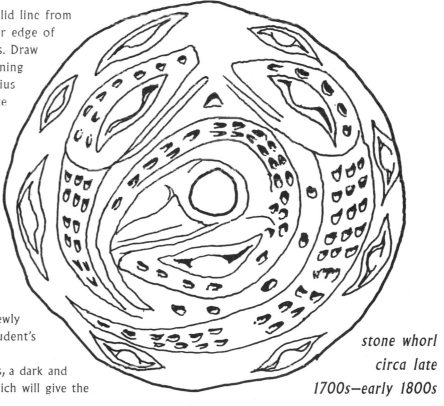

stone whorl
circa late
1700s—early 1800s

The Northwest Coast Indian Art Activity Books

Nan McNutt

This series of fun activity books features the art and culture of Native Americans from Northwest Coastal areas—including the Tlingit, Haida, Tsimshian, Bella Bella, Kwakiutl, and Salish. Each book is reviewed for cultural accuracy by tribal members and uses the work of Northwest Native artists. Activities are field-tested in classrooms, and each volume provides an Adult Teaching Guide. Ages 6-10.

Also of interest—A great resource for Northwest Native culture and travel!

Native Peoples of the Northwest: A Traveler's Guide to Land, Art, & Culture

Jan Halliday and Gail Chehak

In cooperation with the Affiliated Tribes of Northwest Indians

SASQUATCH BOOKS
SEATTLE

Nan McNutt
& Associates

Available at bookstores or order from Sasquatch Books, below:

The Bentwood Box, ISBN 1-57061-116-5, 36 pp, $10.95   qty _____ $_____

The Button Blanket, ISBN 1-57061-118-1, 44 pp, $10.95   _____   _____

The Cedar Plank Mask, ISBN 1-57061-117-3, 36 pp, $10.95   _____   _____

The Spindle Whorl, ISBN 1-57061-115-7, 44pp, $10.95   _____   _____

Native Peoples of the Northwest, ISBN 1-57061-056-8, 256 pp, $16.95   _____   _____

Subtotal   _____   _____

Tax (WA residents only; add 8.6%)   _____

Shipping ($4 for first book, $1 for each additional)   _____

TOTAL   _____

SHIP TO: Name_____   Address _____

City_____   State _____ Zip_____   Phone_____

☐ Check/Money Order enclosed   ☐ Visa   ☐ Mastercard   Account #_____   Exp date _____

Signature _____   Printed name _____   Phone _____

Send order to: Sasquatch Books, 615 Second Ave., Ste. 260, Seattle, WA 98104   (206) 467-4300; Fax (206) 467-4301; Email: books@sasquatchbooks.com

Or **call TOLL-FREE: (800) 775-0817**   Ask for a free catalog of all our Northwest, children's, and Native American titles!